HERO

INVASION OF THE BOTTY SNATCHERS

Steve Barlow · Steve Skidmore
Illustrated by Lee Robinson

EDGE

FRANKLIN WATTS

LONDON·SYDNEY

Franklin Watts
First published in Great Britain in 2018
by The Watts Publishing Group

Text © Steve Barlow and Steve Skidmore 2018
Illustrations © Andrew Tunney 2018
Cover design: Cathryn Gilbert
Executive Editor: Adrian Cole

ISBN 978 1 4451 5927 0
ebook ISBN 978 1 4451 5928 7
Library ebook ISBN 978 1 4451 5929 4

1 3 5 7 9 10 8 6 4 2

Printed in Great Britain

MIX
Paper from
responsible sources
FSC® C104740
www.fsc.org

Franklin Watts
An imprint of
Hachette Children's Group
Part of The Watts Publishing Group
Carmelite House

1

"People of Earth!" squawks the CB radio. "We of the Alien Blob Federation salute you!"

"Huh?" You leap from your seat and twiddle the dials of the radio. "Who is this?"

"I am Grand Blob Squelchi!" says the voice. *"WE COME IN PEACE.* Please respond."

If you want to reply politely to the message, go to 13.

If you think this is a trick, go to 28.

2

You throw a jug of coffee and another jug of hot milk at the aliens.

They **SMACK** their blobby lips. "I like mine with sugar," says one.

"I prefer a caramel latte," says another.

"Get the kid!" orders a third.

Go to 25.

3

"Where are you going?" you ask.

Marcus is terrified. "Anywhere away from those *CRAZY BLOBS!* They aren't getting my

BOTTY!"

Quickly, you open the car door.

"Then you can take my dad with you."

Marcus looks around in panic. "Okay, okay, but hurry!"

You strap your dad into the passenger seat, close the door and step back. Marcus takes off with a squeal of tyres and a cloud of exhaust smoke.

You hope your dad will be safe. Right now you have to think of some way to deal with the blobs. You follow Marcus's car up the ramp, and out onto the street.

Go to 11.

4

You tear into the cycle store. Seconds later you emerge riding a BMX, pedalling for all you're worth.

HOW TO BE A HERO

With most books, you read from the beginning to the end and then stop. You can then read it backwards if you like, but that would be silly.

But in this book, you're the hero. That's why it's called *I Hero*, see?

You read a bit, then you make a choice that takes you to a different part of the book. You might jump from Section 3 to Section 47 or Section 28. Crazy, huh?

If you make a good choice, **GREAT!**

BUUUUUUT...

If you make the wrong choice, **ALL KINDS OF BAD STUFF WILL HAPPEN.**

Hah-ha! Loser! You'll have to start again.

But that won't happen to you, will it?
Because you're not a zero — **YOU'RE A HERO!**

INTRODUCTION

You are the only child of Professor Otto Lunch, the world's leading authority on *ALIEN LIFE FORMS*.

You are used to helping your father and his assistant Marcus in their experiments, and in their attempts to contact aliens via his Cosmic Broadcast (CB) Radio.

You and your father have been *BEAMING* messages to the stars for years, and never had a reply. But, one day, as you are sitting in your dad's lab reading your favourite sci-fi mag, the Cosmic Broadcast machine signals an incoming message

Go to 1.

But the alien flying machines are soon on your tail. They fire! Your botty disintegrates, along with the saddle it was sitting on — and a moment later...

OOOOOOOHHHHHHH!

PUBLISHER'S NOTE: THE REST OF THIS SECTION HAS BEEN CENSORED AS BEING TOO HORRIBLE FOR WORDS, AND IS BEST LEFT TO THE READER'S IMAGINATION.

Go back to 1.

5

You snatch up a gun one of the soldiers has dropped. Ignoring the sergeant's order to bring it back, you yell a terrible war cry and sprint round the corner...

...only to find yourself faced by dozens of blobs, Botty-Gon weapons raised.

Go to 25.

6

You rush into the lab. "Dad, I've found out how..."

Too late, you remember you sent your dad off with Marcus, and the aliens have taken over the lab. They stop ransacking cupboards and drawers, and turn towards you, weapons raised. You aim the toaster at them — but it's unplugged and you've forgotten to load it with sliced bread anyway...

Go to 25.

7

You run from the scene, somehow dodging the terrible effects of the alien weapons.

You make it back to the lab, and find your dad already there. He looks *STUNNED*.

"The aliens were using a Botty-Gon ray!" he whimpers. "Their technology must be centuries ahead of ours! We're facing the end of the world — *BUMAGEDDON!*"

You shake your head. "What a *BUMMER!*"

At that moment, there is a knock at the door.

Through the frosted glass, you can see the shape of *ALIEN BLOBS*.

Your dad squares his shoulders.

"Such powerful beings must be civilised! I must try to reason with them."

If you want to go with your dad, go to 23.

If you want to leave him and run, go to 37.

If you want to knock him out with a tranquiliser shot, go to 19.

8

With your weight slowing it down, Marcus's car will never be able to outrun the flying blobs.

"Go around the corner of the mall," you yell to Marcus, "and stop!"

As the car slows, you vault out of it.

"*GO, GO, GO*!" you yell at Marcus. He accelerates away, and you step back round the corner and wave at the approaching blobs.

"Hey, *uglies*! Here I am!"

The blobs follow you, allowing Marcus to escape. You dodge into a shopping mall, where the alien flying machines can't follow. You've escaped — for the moment!

Go to 11.

9

You sneak out onto the streets until you find a lone **BLOB**. You creep up behind him and let him have it with both bread slots.

You celebrate as the alien screams and vapourises. But you've forgotten that nobody is watching your back. You turn to find three more aliens advancing on you from behind.

Go to 25.

10

"Use your rifles!" you shout.

The soldiers take your advice and fire.

You soon realise that the bullets are just going straight through the aliens' blobby bodies, doing no harm.

"THAT'S NOT WORKING!" you cry.

If you've already made the soldiers use their grenades, go to 36.

If not, go to 21.

11

As you wonder what to do next, a crowd of people running for their lives appears from around the corner. Many of them are holding their botties as they run.

LIKE THAT'S GOING TO DO ANY GOOD, you think.

A squad of soldiers appears, firing their assault rifles in a rearguard action to give the crowd time to escape.

If you want to run away with the crowd, go to 27.

If you want to help the soldiers, go to 41.

12

You look around desperately for something that might stop the aliens. All you can see is the normal stuff you'd find behind the counter in a busy café.

If you want to try stopping the aliens with the coffee machine, go to 2.

If you'd rather try the toaster, go to 26.

If you think you can hold the blobs off with scoops of ice cream, go to 40.

13

"Greetings, Grand Blob Squelchi," you say politely. "What can I do for you?"

"We wish to establish friendly relations with Earth, so that humankind and blobkind can march, and slither, hand in — er — **BLOBBY TENTACLE**, together into a glorious future! We wish to discuss this with the leaders of your world."

"I'll have to ask my dad," you say.

Go to 43.

14

At that moment, **THE ALIENS ATTACK!**

"Watch this!" you cry. You leap in front of the general and fire. The leading aliens are vaporised. The rest flee in panic.

The general points at the toaster. "I want our best men on this!"

Before long, toasters from every kitchen appliance store in the city have been seized by the military and turned into weapons: single shot toasters, semi-automatic toasters, belt-fed toasters.

The new weapons turn the tide. With cries of,

"Eat hot toast, buddy!" the soldiers create havoc in the blobby ranks.

The aliens retreat to their ship, which takes off with a *ROAR!*

To destroy the alien ship, go to 38.

If you want to let the aliens go, turn to 20.

15

You rack your brains. What can soldiers with no botties wear that will stay up? You realise that behind the squad is a onesie store and a swimwear store.

If you want to suggest the soldiers look in the swimwear store, go to 32.

If you want to suggest they visit the onesie store, go to 45.

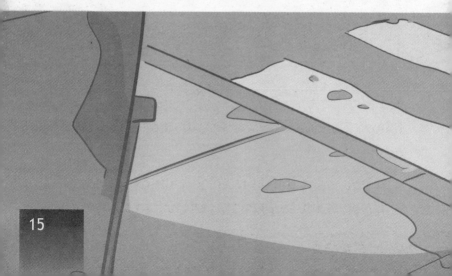

16

You race for the café, but the aliens spot you and follow. They soon have you cornered behind the counter!

If you want to run from the aliens, go to 33.
If you want to fight the aliens, go to 12.

17

The voice on the radio **SPLUTTERS** with indignation.

"How dare you insult the **GLORIOUS** representatives of the Blob Federation?! We will be avenged on your **PUNY** planet!"

If you think you've made a mistake and should apologise, go to 34.

If you think this is a bluff, go to 39.

18

The bottiless defenders' morale is at rock bottom. You encourage them with a rousing speech.

"You have nothing to lose but your botties," you cry, "and you've lost those anyway, so what have you got to lose?"

The soldiers take a few seconds to work this out — but then they set to work fighting the aliens with everything they've got.

It's not enough. The aliens shrug off the attack — and now they unveil a new weapon. A giant flying mirrorball appears, sending coloured lights dancing over the squad and pumping out **FUNK/SOUL** music.

The helpless soldiers drop their weapons and **BOOGIE**.

"It's a dreadful Disco Ray!" you cry, realising the soldiers are losing the battle, and their street cred.

The aliens turn their weapons on you...

Go to 25.

19

Before your dad is halfway to the door, you sneak up behind him and give him a **TRANQUILISER** shot. He stops and his eyes glaze over.

"I'm going to save you from the blobs," you tell him. "Come on, Dad."

As the aliens continue trying to break into the lab, you take him by the hand and lead him to the back door, and down the stairs to the basement garage.

You are almost run over by a speeding two-seater sports car. It screeches to a halt, and your dad's assistant Marcus stares at you from behind the wheel.

If you want to ask Marcus to take your dad to safety, go to 3.

If you want to put your dad in the car and try to escape with him, go to 31.

20

"They're leaving, General," you shout as a cheer goes up from the defenders. "Let them go. Now they know Earth can take care of itself they won't be back in a hurry."

The general scowls at being told what to do, but he gives the order. The ship is soon out of sight.

Go to 50.

"Use your grenades!" you shout.

The soldiers pull the pins from grenades and hurl them at the aliens.

BOOM!

Blobs are blown to bits by the explosions. You and the soldiers cheer!

But the **BLOBBY BITS** immediately start running together, joining to re-form the aliens who are soon as good as new.

"That's no good!" you cry.

If you've already made the soldiers use their rifles, go to 36.

If not, go to 10.

22

You run through panicking crowds until you find the **ONESIE SQUAD**.

"I've found a way to defeat the aliens with a toaster," you tell Sergeant Tiger. "But I'll need a powerful battery and a sliced loaf of bread."

"Sounds **CRAZY**," says the sergeant gruffly, "but what have we got to lose? Corporal Chicken! Private Panda! Find whatever the kid needs."

Soon, the toaster is primed and ready.

If you want to test the toaster yourself, go to 9.

If you want to take the toaster straight to the army chief of staff, go to 30.

23

Your dad opens the door.

"Listen," he says, "I'm sure we're all reasonable people — and blobs. There must be some way we can work this out..."

The blobs are not listening. They advance menacingly into the lab, Botty-Gon weapons at the ready.

"Nooooo!" cries your dad...

Go to 25.

24

You feel some terrible unseen force pass over your head.

VERZOINGGGGGGG!

You hear the soldiers cry out and curse. When you look up, you see to your horror that most of the soldiers in the squad have their combat fatigues and undies around their ankles. Their botties have been snatched! The soldiers can only shuffle a few steps without falling over.

The rest are holding their pants up — but have had to drop their rifles to leave their hands free. They are helpless!

If you want to grab a gun and follow the aliens, go to 5.

If you want to try and help the soldiers, go to 15.

25

The blobs fire!

ZAP! KAPOW! POW!

You feel a sudden chill around your midsection.

You look down and realise in horror that your shirt tails are flapping loose and your jeans and undies are hanging around your ankles.

Desperately, you feel behind you. Your **BOTTY** has disappeared!

That'll teach you not to mess with alien blobs.

Go back to 1.

26

You grab the pop-up toaster. As you do, you realise that someone must have switched it on just before leaving the café. The dial shows the toast is almost done. You hold the toaster out with its slots towards the advancing aliens.

The toaster pings, and toast shoots out. A slice

hits each of the first two aliens. You close your eyes...

ARGHHHHHH!

And open them again, as screams ring around the café. You watch in fascination as the dry toast sucks the blobby juices from the two stricken aliens, who disintegrate into powder. The other aliens flee!

Go to 35.

You turn and run with the crowd.

Alien blobs appear on side streets, or flying alongside the crowd. More panic-stricken people come from every direction to join the stampede. The aliens fire into the mob. Botty-less people scream and fall, brought down by their suddenly unsupported *PANTS* and *UNDIES*. You realise that you are being herded like cattle by the botty-snatching blobs.

If you want to stay with the crowd, go to 47.

If you want to escape and find the soldiers, go to 41.

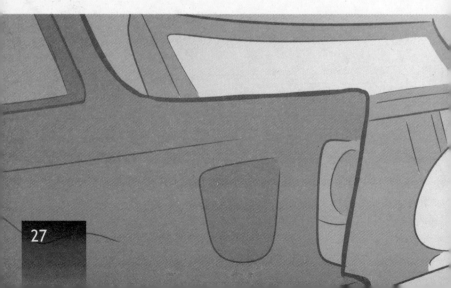

28

"**Yeah?**" you say. "Is this you, **Dwayne**?"

Indignant squawks sound from the radio.

"We do not know this Dwayne of whom you speak. This is Grand Blob Squelchi…"

"Sure it is," you say, "and I'm a martian's grandmother. Get lost, **Dwayne**!"

You hold the microphone in front of your lips and blow the juiciest raspberry you can manage.

PLLLLLPPPPPP!

Go to 17.

29

You race to the greengrocer's with the aliens hard on your heels.

You try to fend off the **BOTTY-THIRSTY BLOBS** with whatever fruit and veg comes to hand. You pelt them with oranges and lemons, kiwis, pineapples and bananas. It's no good. You switch to grape shots using real grapes. Even a watermelon barely slows them down!

Soon the blobs have you cornered by the cabbages and cauliflowers. A leek runs down your leg.

"Leave me in *PEAS!*" you sob, as you think of what might have *BEAN*.

Go to 25.

30

You demonstrate the power of your toaster weapon by **VAPORISING** two aliens that were sneaking up on the **ONESIE SQUAD'S** position.

"Well, I'll be...! Come with me." The sergeant leads you to the general in charge of Earth's defence.

The general listens to what you have to say, but shakes his head. "Sorry, kid. Shooting your enemies full of toast just isn't the army way."

If you want to argue with the general, go to 42.

If you want to demonstrate your weapon's capability, go to 14.

31

"Marcus," you cry, "you've got to help us."

Marcus looks round in panic. "This is a two-seater vehicle! I can't take both of you!"

"Sure you can." You strap your dad into the passenger seat, push it as far forward as it will go, and squeeze into the space behind.

Marcus lets out the clutch. "This is a very bad idea..."

The car surges up the ramp and on to the street. But it is overloaded, and slow.

You look back and realise you are being followed by alien blobs on things that look like flying scooters.

If you want to get out of the car to give the others a chance to escape, go to 8.

If you'd rather stay in the car, go to 44.

32

"I've got a great idea!" you tell the soldiers. You point at the swimwear store. "You can wear swimsuits!"

"How are we going to keep swimming trunks up with no botties?" demands one.

"Yeah, or bikinis?" asks another.

"You could try mankinis," you say. The soldiers glare at you. "Or even better," you say quickly, pointing at the other store, "**ONESIES**!"

Go to 45.

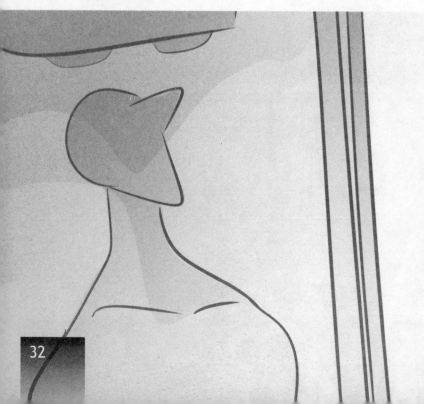

33

You spot a door behind the counter. It leads to the kitchen. You race through it, scattering pots, pans and cutlery in all directions, and tear through the back door...

...only to run straight into a whole heap of aliens who were expecting you to do exactly what you've just done. They have you covered; there is no escape.

Go to 25.

34

"Hey, hold on," you say. "Look, I'm sorry. I thought one of my friends was playing a joke."

"Very well," says the voice. "We accept your apology. But watch it, next time."

If you really are making *FIRST CONTACT* with aliens, you decide you'd better be extra-specially polite.

Go to 13.

35

You run out of the café, clutching the toaster to your chest. Purely by chance, you have found a

weapon that might defeat the alien menace.
But where should you go now?

If you want to go back to the lab, go to 6.
If you want to take your discovery to the army, go to 22.

36

"Cease your fire!" you tell the soldiers. "You're just wasting ammunition."

Sergeant Tiger **GROWLS** in frustration.

"There must be some way we can beat them!"

Before you can reply, scores of blob reinforcements appear.

If you want to stand and fight, go to 18.
If you would rather make a strategic withdrawal, go to 48.

37

"They won't listen!" you tell your dad. "We've got to run..."

Your dad ignores you and reaches for the door handle.

In a flash, you are out of the window. You hear a shriek of embarrassment behind you as the aliens deprive your dad of his botty.

You race around the corner — straight into a squad of alien blobs. Before you can escape, they raise their weapons...

Go to 25.

38

"General, call in the Air Force," you cry. **"DESTROY THAT SHIP!"**

"Who's in charge around here?" demands the general. But he gives the order anyway.

Jets appear and fire missiles at the retreating ship, but it is protected by a force field and they have no effect.

Every radio in the vicinity crackles into life.

"EARTHLINGS!" cries an alien voice. "You have tried to destroy us all! You show us no mercy — so we will show you none!"

Go to 46.

39

"Yeah, right," you say, "you're really aliens, and you come from outer space and you zip around in *FLYING SAUCERS* and you're really going to blow up the world, **oh boo hoo**, I'm so scared."

"That's right," says the voice on the radio. "Prepare to meet your doom, Earthling."

"Drop dead," you say. "Put an egg in your shoe and beat it."

Go to 46.

40

You pelt the aliens with scoops of ice cream. They grow blobby tongues to lick it off.

"Vanilla? Boring!" says one.

"I've got pistachio," says another. "Tasty!"

"Get the kid!" orders a third.

You thought you could fight off aliens with pistachio ice cream? Are you nuts?

Go to 25.

41

You break away from the crowd. You've done enough running — it's time to stand and fight!

Moments later, you are surrounded by soldiers. Their faces are tense as they fire at the oncoming blobs.

The sergeant in charge of the squad glares at you.

"What are you doing here?" he shouts.

"I want to fight!" you yell back.

The sergeant makes no reply — instead, he pushes you roughly to the ground.

Go to 24.

42

You can't believe that this boneheaded brass-hat would rather face defeat by the aliens than change his mind about fighting tactics.

"But, General," you cry, "this is the only way to defeat..."

You get no further. A swarm of aliens descends on their flying scooters. Alien ground troops advance at maximum **WOBBLE**. The command post is overrun. You load your toaster and fire, but you don't have time to let the toast get nicely brown and the underdone slices have no effect. Soon you are surrounded.

Go to 18.

You rush off and tell your dad about the alien message.

A week later, the leaders of the world are gathered at the local airport to welcome the alien ship as it lands. You have joined the crowds with your dad and his assistant Marcus.

A ramp descends from the ship and a band of alien blobs squelches down it. They are playing instruments that look like futuristic bagpipes and making a terrible racket. The world leaders look at each other uneasily.

A spokesblob approaches the microphone.

"PEOPLE OF EARTH," it bellows, "THANK YOU FOR GATHERING ALL YOUR LEADERS HERE. IT WILL MAKE OUR INVASION OF YOUR PLANET SO MUCH EASIER."

The blob turns to the 'band'.

You realise that the band's instruments are weapons. There is chaos as the aliens fire into the crowd. Everywhere the blobs point their weapons, trousers, skirts and undies drop to the ground!

If you want to run from the alien menace, go to 7.

If you want to try and reason with the aliens, go to 49.

44

"Keep going!" you cry. "I'll try and slow them down!"

Marcus has a few tools scattered on the floor behind the seats. You pick these up one by one and stand to hurl them at the pursuing blobs. A wheel brace strikes one scooter, which trails smoke and crashes into a doughnut stand. But the other blobs avoid your primitive missiles and draw alongside, weapons raised.

Go to 25.

45

You lead the soldiers into the onesie store. There are lots of colourful outfits on display — *bunny rabbit onesies, tiger onesies, panda onesies, crocodile onesies...*

The soldiers look around in horror.

"We can't wear these!" says the sergeant in disgust. "We'll look ridiculous!"

You look him straight in the eye. Well, it's better than looking further down!

"More ridiculous than you do now?"

"Fair point, well made," says the sergeant.

"Okay men, choose a onesie — but I get the tiger!"

Soon all the soldiers are dressed in onesies. Obviously, with no botties they can't wear their undies — so they're **COMMANDOES** going **COMMANDO!**

"Let's go," says the sergeant. "Time to kick alien butt."

"They're blobs," you say, "I'm not sure they have **BUTTS**."

"Well, whatever they have," growls the sergeant, "we'll **kick** that! Check your weapons."

The soldiers run out of the store just as a platoon of alien blobs appear round the corner.

If you think the soldiers should use their rifles to attack the aliens, go to 10.

If you think they should use grenades, go to 21.

46

There is a brief flash of blinding light in the sky, and moments later your body is blown into a random collection of atoms — along with the rest of the Earth.

It's a bad idea to provoke alien life forms of unknown capabilities.

Go back to 1.

47

You realise that the people in front of you have stopped running. All around you, voices are raised in alarm.

You look up to see that the blobs have herded the crowd into a delivery area surrounded on three sides by high walls. There is no way out!

The aliens advance on all sides, their terrible Botty-Gon weapons at the ready.

Go to 25.

48

"*RUN AWAY!*" you yell. "Every cute kitten, cuddly squirrel and purple unicorn for himself!"

The soldiers scatter quickly. Desperately, you look around for somewhere to hide.

A little way down the street you see a café and, next to that, a greengrocer's, while across the way is a bicycle store.

If you want to hide in the café, go to 16.

If you want to seek shelter in the greengrocer's, go to 29.

If you'd rather make for the bicycle store, go to 4.

You step forward, waving your arms.

"Stop! Stop! I'm the one you spoke to on the radio. You said you came in peace and I..."

The aliens turn their weapons on you.

OO-ER, you think, *BAD MISTAKE...*

If you want to run, go to 7.

If you refuse to show fear, and decide to stand your ground, go to 25.

50

The entire army, and everyone in the city all want to congratulate you.

By the time you get back to the lab, your dad is already there, and the tranquiliser you gave him has worn off.

"We'll have words about that later," he growls, "but right now, you can help me with my new invention."

"What new invention?" you ask.

"Something to help all those poor people with no botties! I call it my **Butt Restora Ray**..."

You sigh. To the people of Planet Earth, you're a big hero! *TO YOUR DAD...*

...NOT SO MUCH.

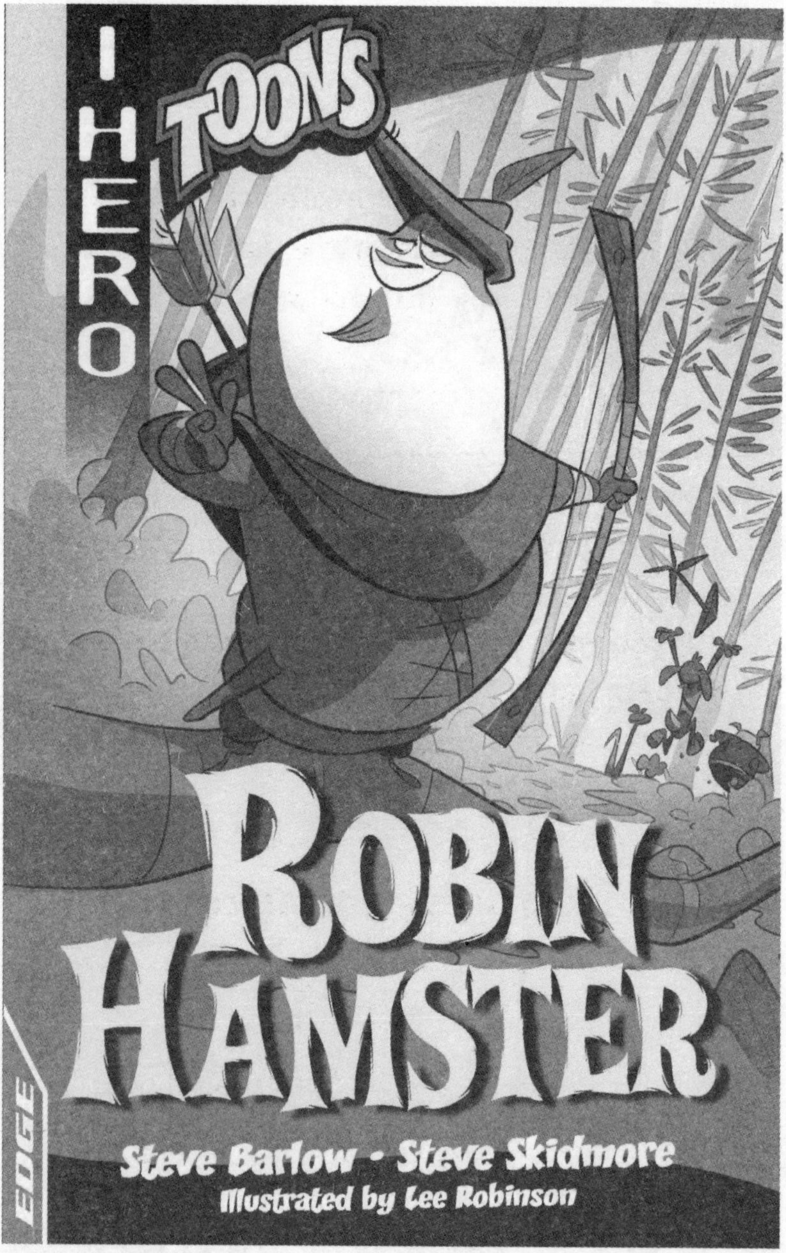
I HERO
TOONS
ROBIN HAMSTER
Steve Barlow · Steve Skidmore
Illustrated by Lee Robinson
EDGE

You are Robin Hamster, the leader of a band of outlaws. You live in the greenwood. You fight for good and justice for all.

You have sworn to fight to protect the weak and helpless. You steal from the rich and give to the poor (and keep a little for yourself!).

You are hiding in the branches of a great oak tree waiting for the tax collector.

You see him coming down the track. His wagon is pulled by two horses. You have several ways to spring the ambush.

If you wish to chop down a tree to block the path, go to 26.

If you wish to swing on a rope and land on the wagon, go to 18.

Continue the adventure in:

About the 2Steves

"The 2Steves" are
Britain's most popular
writing double act
for young people,
specialising in comedy
and adventure. They
perform regularly in schools and libraries,
and at festivals, taking the power of words
and story to audiences of all ages.

Together they have written many books,
including the *I HERO Immortals* and *iHorror* series.

About the illustrator: Lee Robinson

Lee studied animation at Newcastle College and
went on to work on comics such as *Kung Fu
Panda*, as well as running comicbook workshops
throughtout the northeast of England. When he's
not drawing, Lee loves running, reading and video
games. He now lives in Edmonton, Canada, where
he's got plenty of time to come up with crazy ideas
while waiting for the weather to warm up.

I HERO Legends — collect them all!

ATHENA

978 1 4451 5234 9 pb
978 1 4451 5235 6 ebook

BEOWULF

978 1 4451 5225 7 pb
978 1 4451 5226 4 ebook

KING ARTHUR

978 1 4451 5231 8 pb
978 1 4451 5232 5 ebook

FREYA

978 1 4451 5237 0 pb
978 1 4451 5238 7 ebook

HERCULES

978 1 4451 5228 8 pb
978 1 4451 5229 5 ebook

ROBIN HOOD

978 1 4451 5183 0 pb
978 1 4451 5184 7 ebook

Have you read the I HERO Monster Hunter series?

ALIEN

978 1 4451 5878 5 pb
978 1 4451 5876 1 ebook

GHOST

978 1 4451 5939 3 pb
978 1 4451 5940 9 ebook

MUTANT

978 1 4451 5943 4 pb
978 1 4451 5946 1 ebook

VAMPIRE

978 1 4451 5936 2 pb
978 1 4451 5937 9 ebook

WEREWOLF

978 1 4451 5942 3 pb
978 1 4451 5943 0 ebook

ZOMBIE

978 1 4451 5935 5 pb
978 1 4451 5933 1 ebook

Also by the 2Steves...

978 1 4451 5104 5 pb
978 1 4451 5119 9 eBook

You are a skilled, stealthy ninja. Your village has been attacked by a warlord called Raiden. Now YOU must go to his castle and stop him before he destroys more lives.

978 1 4451 5101 4 pb
978 1 4451 5117 5 eBook

You are the Warrior Princess. Someone wants to steal the magical ice diamonds from the Crystal Caverns. YOU must discover who it is and save your kingdom.

978 1 4451 5103 8 pb
978 1 4451 5121 2 eBook

You are a magical unicorn. Empress Yin Yang has stolen Carmine, the red unicorn. Yin Yang wants to destroy the colourful Rainbow Land. YOU must stop her!

978 1 4451 5102 1 pb
978 1 4451 5124 3 eBook

You are a spy, codenamed Scorpio. Someone has taken control of secret satellite laser weapons. YOU must find out who is responsible and stop their dastardly plans.